Order this book online at www.trafford.com
or email orders@trafford.com

Most Trafford titles are also available at major online book retailers.

© Copyright 2016 Michael McWade .

Print information available on the last page.

ISBN: 978-1-4907-7584-5(sc)
ISBN: 978-1-4907-7583-8 (e)

Library of Congress Control Number: 2016912494

Because of the dynamic nature of the Internet, any web addresses or links contained in this book may have changed since publication and may no longer be valid. The views expressed in this work are solely those of the author and do not necessarily reflect the views of the publisher, and the publisher hereby disclaims any responsibility for them.

Our mission is to efficiently provide the world's finest, most comprehensive book publishing service, enabling every author to experience success. To find out how to publish your book, your way, and have it available worldwide, visit us online at www.trafford.com

Any people depicted in stock imagery provided by Thinkstock are models, and such images are being used for illustrative purposes only. Certain stock imagery © Thinkstock.

Trafford rev. 08/22/2016

www.trafford.com
North America & international
toll-free: 1 888 232 4444 (USA & Canada)
phone: 250 383 6864 ✦ fax: 812 355 4082

Dedication

I want to dedicate this story to all the parents and guardians who will never get a chance to read it to a child. Whether through illness or senseless violence, they have been deprived the chance to share many life experiences, including reading, with them.

"If you want to survive in this world, you must pay more attention to everything around you."

LaKisha's World

The Birds in my Yard

Michael McWade

LaKisha looked out her bedroom window. "Mom, what kind of birds are those?"
LaKisha's mom entered the room, put her
arm around her daughter's shoulder, and said,
"Those are cardinals, my dear."

"What are they doing?" asked LaKisha.
"They are building a nest," said LaKisha's mom.
LaKisha's eyes got real wide, "They're going
to have babies?" asked LaKisha anxiously.

"Yes, I hope so."

"That would be awesome!" LaKisha looked up at her
mom. "Why is one of the cardinals really bright red and
the other one kind of brown?"

"The bright red one is the daddy cardinal and the brown
one is the mama cardinal" said LaKisha's mom.

"I thought girls were prettier than boys," said LaKisha.

LaKisha's mom gave a little chuckle. "Well, my dear, in most animals the boys are naturally more colorful
than the girls."

LaKisha gave her mom a weird look and smiled, "Is that why Daddy doesn't have to wear makeup and
you do?"

LaKisha's mom just gave her a pat on the head, sighed and turned to look out the window to watch the birds
busily making their nest.

****

Mama Cardinal was so excited.
This was the day she had been waiting for,
and her eggs were about to hatch.
"Now calm down Mama," said
Daddy Cardinal. "They're not going to hatch
any faster with you standing over them."

"I'm just so excited. These will be our first children," said
Mama Cardinal.

Suddenly, one of the eggs began to move ever so slightly.
It rocked back and forth just a little bit, and then a crack
appeared.

The crack got wider and wider and soon a little baby bird's head appeared.

"Oh!" shouted Mama Cardinal. The little baby bird struggled to get itself out of the egg. Mama Cardinal, who was sitting on the edge of the nest, moved forward to help the little bird. "No, Mama," said Daddy Cardinal as he put a wing out to hold her back, "he needs to do this by himself."

The baby bird made one last push, and out of the egg he came! Daddy Cardinal beamed with pride, and Mama Cardinal had tears in her eyes. Before they knew it, the other two eggs began to wiggle as well. The second baby bird took no time getting out of the egg, but the last one seemed to be struggling.

They could see the baby bird's head,
but the harder he pushed, he still
wasn't able to free himself from the egg.
He looked up at Mama Cardinal and
Daddy Cardinal with sad eyes, as if to say,
"help me." Daddy Cardinal gave a worried
look to Mama Cardinal and reached

down to pull the egg shells away from the third baby bird.

Once he had finished he gave a heavy sigh and looked up at Mama Cardinal. Mama Cardinal looked down into the nest. "Oh, dear," she said. The last baby bird only had one leg!

****

It was a beautiful sunny day as LaKisha was looking look out the window of her room again. Her mom had just put out a bird feeder in their yard and there was all kinds of activity.

"Mom," she said, "hurry, come quick. Look at all the birds in our yard! What kinds are they?"

LaKisha's mom began pointing to the different birds and said, "Well, those small brown ones are called sparrows. Those gold-ish yellow ones are called finches. Those big black ones are Crows. Those orangish-brown ones are robins and that big blue-and-white one with the pointy head is called a blue jay. They are mean, and the other birds don't really like them very much."

LaKisha suddenly got very excited and pointed to the cardinal's nest, "Look, the eggs are hatching!"

She watched as the first and second baby birds crawled out of the eggs. "What's wrong with the last one?" she asked. "I'm not sure," said LaKisha's mom as she looked on intensely.

As the last baby bird emerged from its egg, LaKisha gave out a little yell, "Oh, it only has one leg!" LaKisha's mom put her arm around her daughter and said, "Sometimes that happens in nature, sweetie. I hope he makes the best of it."

LaKisha looked up at her mom, smiled and said, "I bet he will. I'm going to call him Onesie, and he's my favorite bird in the yard."

****

Onesie was sitting on the tree branch looking a little sad. A little bird, one he had never seen before in the yard - flew up and sat down beside him. "Hi!" the little bird said. Onesie, glad to have a little company, said to the new bird, "What kind of bird are you?"

"I'm a warbler. My name is Jake. So, Red, you don't mind if I call you Red, do you?" Onesie shook his head no. "Well, Red, why so sad?" asked his new found friend. Onesie gave a heavy sigh and said, "My brothers are out practicing their flying but I can't because of my disability." He held out his one leg to show the warbler.

"Wow, that's a bummer" said the warbler. "But I'll bet I could teach you to fly."

"You could? Do you think you really could?" said Onesie hopefully. "Sure" said Jake, "all you have to do is..."

The tree branch they were on suddenly shook, and they turned to see that Daddy Cardinal had landed next to them. "What are you doing here, and why are you talking to my son?" he said as he glared at the warbler. Jake began to say something when Daddy Cardinal said, "Shoo, off with you now!" Jake bolted from the tree branch and was gone.

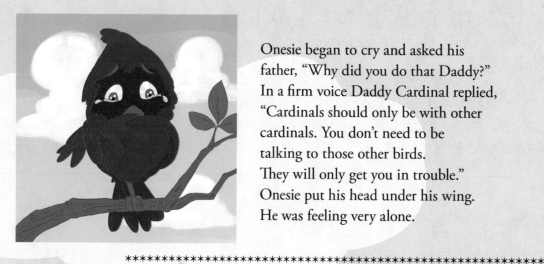

Onesie began to cry and asked his father, "Why did you do that Daddy?" In a firm voice Daddy Cardinal replied, "Cardinals should only be with other cardinals. You don't need to be talking to those other birds. They will only get you in trouble." Onesie put his head under his wing. He was feeling very alone.

****

LaKisha was sitting at the kitchen table with her mother, "Mom," she asked, "now that Mama Cardinal and Daddy Cardinal have babies will they get married?" LaKisha's mom just smiled and said, "No honey, birds don't get married like humans do. But most of them do stay together for their whole lives so it's kind of like marriage. It's called monogamy."

"Mo-nahg-a-me," repeated LaKisha. LaKisha went outside to fill up the bird feeder as her mom had told her to do, then sat in the chair on her porch. She noticed the one-legged bird sitting on the tree branch. "Hi, Onesie" she said, "How are you today?"

The one-legged bird looked up at LaKisha and just shrugged. "Are you hungry?" LaKisha took a handful of the bird seed that she just put in the feeder and put some on a flat part of the branch next to the one-legged bird. "Here, this will make you feel better."

Onesie began to eat the food hungrily. LaKisha was so excited she ran into the house, yelling, "Mommy! Mommy! I just fed Onesie some food and he ate it!"

****

Onesie was eating the bird seed that LaKisha had given him when the branch shook ever so slightly. He looked up and saw the warbler sitting next to him. "You're not supposed to be here. I can get in trouble."

"I waited until your father had gone away, so it should be safe. Besides, Red, I promised to teach you how to fly."

"Do you really think you could?" asked Onesie.

"Sure," said Jake, "it's all a matter of balance." So the little golden warbler showed Onesie how to position his body on a slight angle - and if he did, then he should be able to fly. "I don't know," said Onesie. "I'm kind of nervous."

Jake gave him a nudge and said, "Oh, don't be such a baby and just try it." Onesie was very happy just to have somebody to talk to while his brothers were all out flying, and to have a new friend that he flapped his wings and jumped off the branch, flopping around and then immediately hitting the ground. "Ouch!" he said. "That hurt."

"Well, you're just going to have to keep on trying till you get it right," said Jake.

So Onesie tried and tried over and over again. He was just about ready to give up when he felt the wind under his wings, and suddenly, he was flying! "Woo-hoo!" yelled Onesie.

He was so happy he flew off the branch and onto the roof of the house. And then around and around the yard he went without a care in the world for the first time in his life.

In the distance, he saw his brothers and he couldn't wait to fly over and show them his newfound flying skills. What he didn't notice was that he was about to cross the street, and a big, giant truck was coming right at him.

****

LaKisha grabbed her mom's arm and dragged her into the back yard. "Quick, Mama, I gave Onesie some food and now look - he's flying!" The two watched as Onesie looped and looped around the yard and suddenly he darted into the street, the giant truck getting ever closer to him. LaKisha screamed "Oh, no!" Her mom covered her eyes with her hands.

****

Mama Cardinal had been gathering food and water for her family's next meal when she heard loud noises coming from the backyard. At that moment, Daddy Cardinal landed next to her and said, "What's all that racket going on in the yard?" They flew around to the side of the house and looked up. There was Onesie, happily flying around. They saw him start to cross the street as the truck was about to hit him but they were too far away to help.
"Oh" said Mama Cardinal as she looked at Daddy Cardinal with fear in her eyes.

The big, giant truck was just about to hit Onesie when out of nowhere came a streak of something that knocked him out of the way of the truck. It was Jake! The little warbler had saved Onesie's life!

LaKisha jumped up and down and began cheering, and Mama Cardinal gave Daddy Cardinal a big hug and a kiss.

Onesie, who was on the ground, was a little groggy as he looked up and saw his friends and family all looking down at him. "What happened?" he said. Jake looked down at his friend, smiled and said, "I just saved your butt because you weren't paying attention to where you were going."

Mama Cardinal gave Onesie a big hug and said, "Oh, my dear, you had me so worried." Daddy Cardinal took a deep breath and looked at Jake, his face was redder than his feathers. "Well, warbler, I guess you're not so bad after all. My son is lucky to have a friend like you." Then he turned to Onesie and said, "And you young man, you can continue your flying practice but in the back yard only - got it?"

Onesie smiled and then nodded at his friend with a big thank you on his face.

LaKisha watched from the window in her room as all the birds got up and flew back into the trees in her yard. "All this activity from just the birds in my yard," she thought. "I'll have to keep watching. You never know what else is out there."

THE END

Printed in the United States
By Bookmasters